JUSTICE LEAGUE

HOW TO DRAW

SCHOLASTIC INC.

New York   Toronto London   Auckland   Sydney
Mexico City   New Delhi   Hong Kong   Buenos Aires

ISBN 0-439-57167-7

Published by Scholastic Inc.
SCHOLASTIC and associated logos are trademarks and/or registered trademarks of Scholastic Inc.

12 11 10 9 8 7 6 5 4 3   3 4 5 6 7 8/0

Designed by Ursula Albano
Printed in the U.S.A.
First printing, October 2003

Introduction

When interstellar invaders and world-conquering super-villains threaten the earth, more than one super hero may be needed to battle the threat. That's when the call goes out to the Justice League. Superman, Batman, Wonder Woman, Green Lantern, the Flash, Hawkgirl, and Martian Manhunter together are the Justice League, united in the fight for truth, justice, and freedom.

Now you can learn to draw these super heroes and create your own adventures by following the steps in this book. Here's what you'll need:

1. Sharp pencils
2. Colored pencils or markers
3. An eraser
4. Graph paper

Okay, got all that? Then you're ready to start. Just follow the step-by-step drawings in this book. Copy the lines in each step onto your graph paper. Notice where the lines touch the grid—and where they don't! Keep your arm loose and relaxed as you draw. Finally, have fun! That's all there is to it.

SUPERMAN

Sent to Earth from the exploding planet Krypton, Superman was raised by Jonathan and Martha Kent, who named him Clark. After traveling for many years, Clark Kent moved to Metropolis, where he became a reporter at the *Daily Planet* newspaper. His role as a journalist has alerted him to thousands of emergencies over the years. And as Superman he has fought tirelessly to defend Earth and protect all people.

Superman's ability to fly allows him to speed to any scene where his special powers may be needed.

BATMAN

Bruce Wayne saw his parents killed in front of him and, from that day forward, he dedicated his life to eradicating crime. Trained to the peak of physical and mental perfection, Batman stands guard over Gotham City and, when duty calls, the World's Greatest Detective joins forces with the heroes of the Justice League to fight for justice throughout the world.

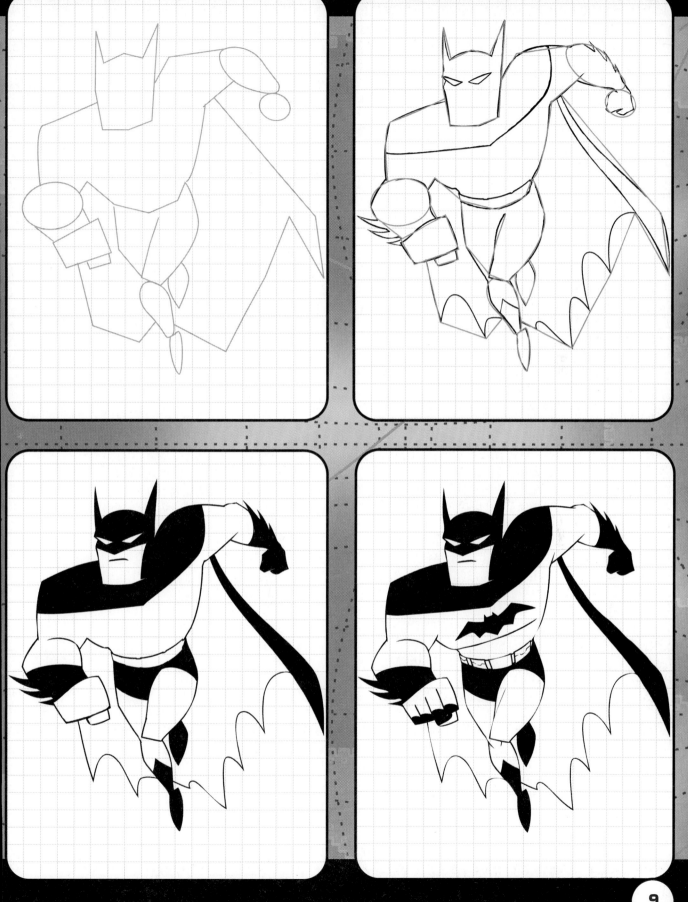

BATMAN

In this pose, Batman is ready to spring into action against any enemy.

WONDER WOMAN

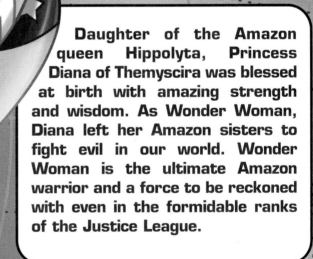

Daughter of the Amazon queen Hippolyta, Princess Diana of Themyscira was blessed at birth with amazing strength and wisdom. As Wonder Woman, Diana left her Amazon sisters to fight evil in our world. Wonder Woman is the ultimate Amazon warrior and a force to be reckoned with even in the formidable ranks of the Justice League.

JUSTICE LEAGUE

WONDER WOMAN

In this pose, Wonder Woman is using her magic bracelets. These bracelets can deflect objects thrown at her. They are one of the many tools that Wonder Woman can call upon when danger threatens.

MARTIAN MANHUNTER

The last survivor of an ancient Martian race, J'onn J'onzz is one of the mightiest heroes on Earth, a telepath with uncanny shape-shifting abilities, the power to pass through solid objects, and incredible strength. The Martian Manhunter is a loner, an outsider fascinated by the contradictions of the human mind. But when danger strikes, the Martian Manhunter steps forward to face the challenge as a member of the Justice League.

GREEN LANTERN

The immortal Guardians of the planet Oa granted Earthman John Stewart the Power Ring of the elite Green Lantern Corps. An intergalactic peacekeeping force, members of the corps wield the ultimate defensive weapon, a ring that responds to their thoughts to project powerful laserlike beams or impenetrable force fields. Green Lantern has proven himself the ultimate weapon in the force for good, in the Justice League.

JUSTICE LEAGUE™

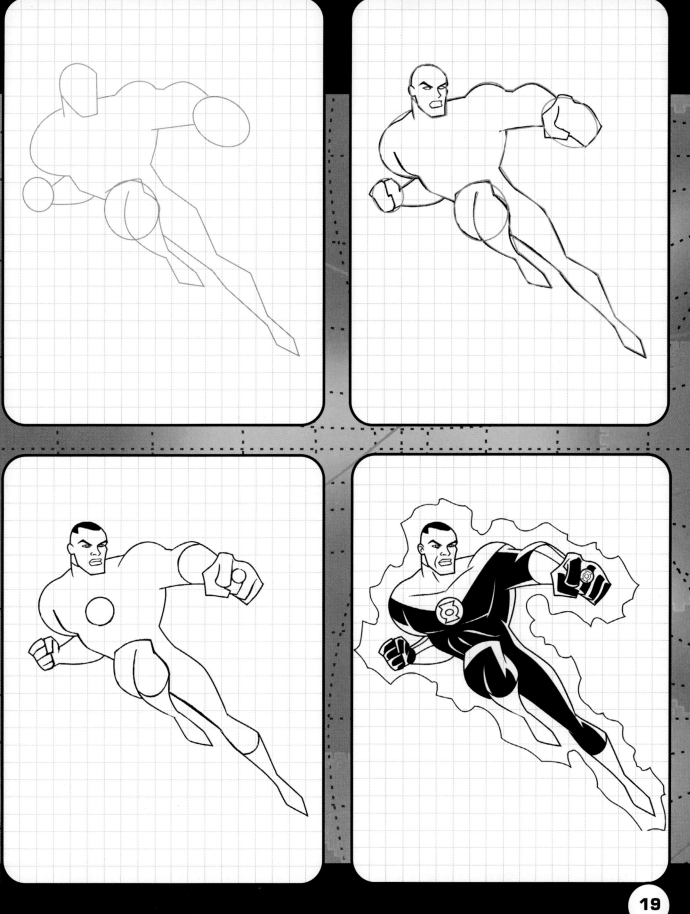

THE FLASH

Young, brash, and impulsive, Wally West gained the power of superspeed during a freak electrochemical accident. Now the Flash is the Fastest Man Alive, capable of speeds approaching that of light. But even if he often acts before he thinks, the Flash is the first one to race into the fight . . . and the superspeeding winner in many a race against doom with the Justice League.

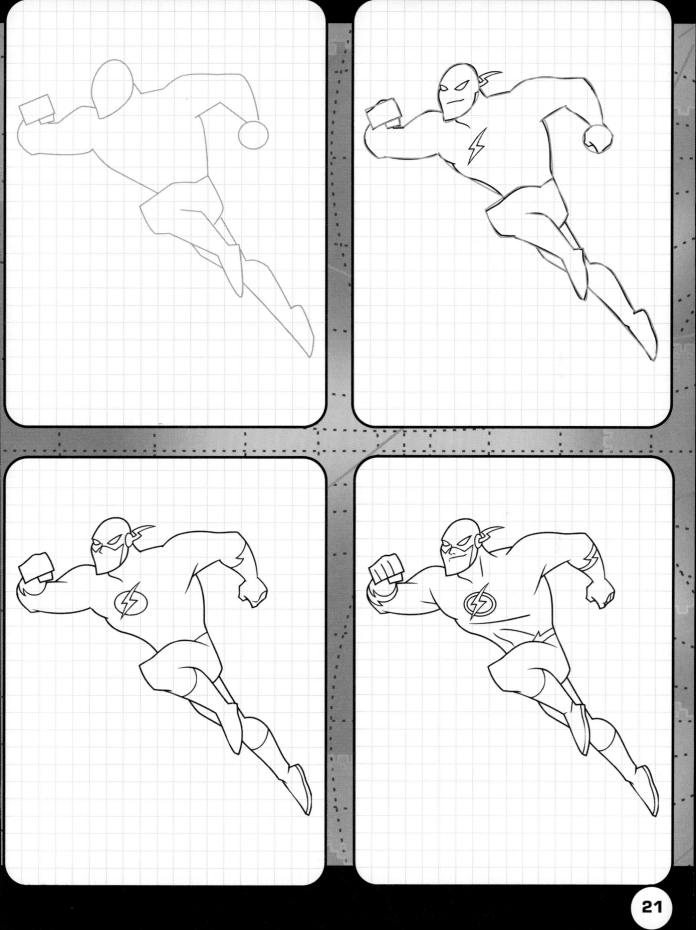

HAWKGIRL

Ripped from her home world of Thanagar, undercover detective Shayera Hol found herself transported to the uncharted planet called Earth. In order to blend in with people, Shayera adopted two identities—that of an ordinary human and that of Hawkgirl. As Hawkgirl, Shayera uses her powers of flight, hand-to-hand combat skills, and the ability to communicate with birds to fight alongside the Justice League.

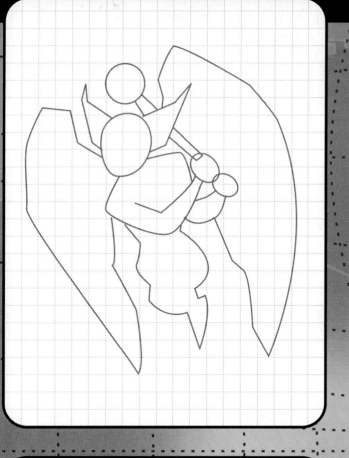

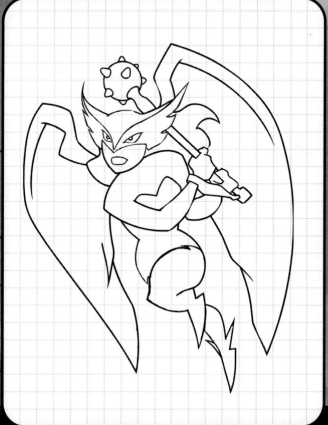

JUSTICE LEAGUE

The Justice League—a collection of the world's greatest super heroes and Earth's first—and last—line of defense when danger threatens the planet.

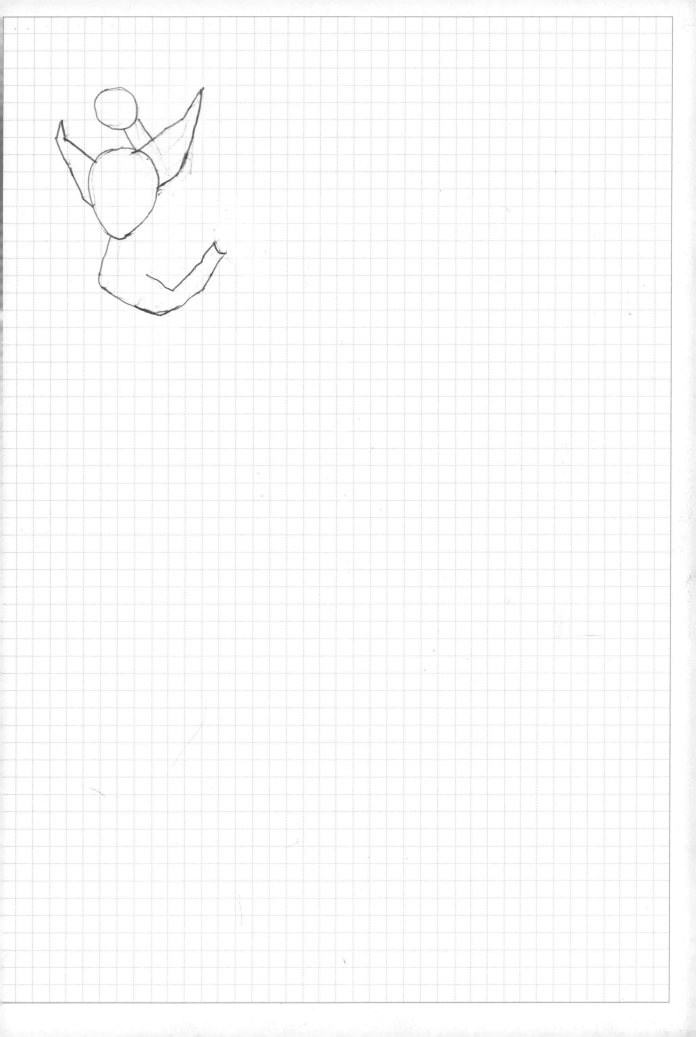